Give the Dog a Bone

ALLAN AHLBERG · ANDRE AMSTUTZ

MAMMOTH

On a dark dark hill
in a dark dark garden
there is a little bony dog . . .

without a bone.

This little dog,
all alone,
sits in his kennel
and dreams of a bone.

One night, the dog skeleton
goes for a walk all by himself
in the dark dark street.
Suddenly, he sees an old friend –
and chases her.

This little dog
chases a cat,
hits a tree
and falls down flat.

The dog skeleton
loses a bit of himself
but keeps walking.
He comes to the dark dark park
and swings on the swings
and slides on the slide.

He chases the ducks
on the dark dark pond . . .
and loses another bit!

This little dog
chases a duck,
loses a leg –
what rotten luck!

The dog skeleton
hops out of the dark dark park,
down the dark dark street
and into the dark dark pet shop.

Suddenly, he sees some more old friends . . .

and they chase <u>him</u>.

This little dog
slips and slides.
Can anyone here
see where he hides?

Off goes the dog,
away from the pet shop,
away from the pets
and away from himself.
(He's lost another bit!)

The dog skeleton
hops up the street
and over the hill
and down the street
and round the corner.

Suddenly, he meets another old friend . . . and plays with him.

This little dog
    chases a friend,
loses his tail –
    is this the end?

FOG!

Bits of him gone.
Lost in the fog.
Can anyone see
what's left of the dog?

No, they can't.
The big skeleton
on his bike can't,
and the little <u>skeleton</u>
on his bike can't.
Look out!

This little dog
    howls and groans.
There he is now,
    just a pile of bones.

But not for long.
Soon the big skeleton
and the little skeleton
gather him up.

They follow the trail
of his lost bones,
along the street,
into the pet shop,
into the park . . .
and back home.

Then they put him together again.

"His legs are on wrong," says Little.

"Wofo!" barks the dog.

"His tail is on wrong," says Big.

"Owof!" barks the dog.

"His head is on wrong," say Little <u>and</u> Big.

"Foow!" barks the dog.

At last the dog skeleton
is himself again.
"Woof-woof!" he barks,
and trots off on <u>four</u> legs
to his kennel.

On a dark dark hill
in a dark dark garden
there is a little bony dog . . .

The End

First published in Great Britain 1993
by William Heinemann Ltd
Published 1994 by Mammoth
an imprint of Reed Books Ltd
Michelin House, 81 Fulham Road, London SW3 6RB
and Auckland, Melbourne, Singapore and Toronto

Reprinted 1994 (twice), 1995 (twice), 1996

ISBN 0 7497 1671 1

A CIP catalogue record for this title
is available from the British Library

Printed in Great Britain
by Scotprint Ltd, Musselburgh